JUSTICE LEAGUE

Speed Trap

JUSTICE LEAGUE

Speed Trap

by

BRIAN AUGUSTYN

Based on a story idea
by Rich Fogel and Andrew Kreisberg

BANTAM BOOKS
NEW YORK • TORONTO • LONDON • SYDNEY • AUCKLAND

SPEED TRAP

A Bantam Book/November 2003

ISBN: 0-553-48780-9

Visit us on the Web! www.randomhouse.com/kids
Educators and librarians, for a variety of teaching tools, visit us at
www.randomhouse.com/teachers

Visit DC Comics at www.dccomics.com

Published simultaneously in the United States and Canada

Bantam Books is an imprint of Random House Children's Books, a division of
Random House, Inc. BANTAM BOOKS and the rooster colophon are registered
trademarks of Random House, Inc.

PRINTED IN THE UNITED STATES OF AMERICA

OPM   10 9 8 7 6 5 4 3 2 1

11/03
B4

Dedicated to Nadine, Carolyn, and Allie, with love.

Thanks to Julie Schwartz,
Carmine Infantino, and my
editor, Paul Kupperberg.

PROLOGUE

Slaughter Creek was the hard part of Central City, even for the seasoned outlaws who responded to the strange summons on that wet evening. Everything in the Creek seemed to be in ruin, and what little light could be found came from the lurid, buzzing neon signs in the dirty windows of the corner saloon. As the eight men made their way past buckled, potholed pavement and burned-out shops, none of them could shake the feeling that they were traversing the heart of a war zone. They weren't far wrong; many battles had been fought here over the years. To date there had been no winners.

Despite their collective experience as practitioners of the criminal arts (for such is how this elite group defined themselves), this no-man's-land made them more than a bit nervous. There were no banks to rob here. No jewelry stores to plunder. No costumed heroes to taunt.

Down here, police response time averaged somewhere between forget it and not a chance. It was the perfect place, the desperados understood, for the bizarre summit to which they had been called.

One by one the wary bandits made their way to the venue for their mysterious meeting: the boarded-up and ramshackle Keystone Theater. The building's gilding and paint had long since peeled, its art deco ornamentation water-stained and crumbling. The last film shown there, according to the tattered, faded poster still on display, had been a war film entitled *The Losers*. That had been twenty-five years ago.

One by one, the eight visitors passed through the moldy and decaying lobby, heading toward the flickering light in the auditorium beyond.

"Anyone for Raisinets?" said the slim blond man with the crooked grin.

"Zip it, Jesse," said the man with the Crocodile Hunter accent and the boomerang-print tie. "D'you really want to mess with a blighter who can call this many of us together on a whim?"

"Who exactly is this guy?" asked the blond man.

A booming basso profundo rang out from the auditorium.

"Come in, everyone. My time is precious!" The voice seemed to make the very air around them vibrate, shaking something deep inside every one of them.

"Whoever he is," said the Aussie with an audible gulp, "I suddenly wish I'd been busy tonight."

The eight nervous outlaws took seats in the dilapidated theater. On the screen, bright color swirled and sparkled, revealing only the hazy projected silhouette of the one who had summoned them. He was big, but nothing more than that could be discerned.

The voice that rang in the large hall had to be mechanically filtered; there was no way what they heard emanated from a human throat. Whoever the voice belonged to, though, he had a rapt audience.

"My terms are final and absolute," he said. "There will be no discussion and no negotiation."

The cowed criminals nodded assent.

The commanding voice continued. "In exchange for one simple action taken on my behalf, I will make available to you an arsenal of unique weapons—devices far beyond anything human technology can hope to duplicate."

"Who do we have to kill?" asked the man known as Jesse.

"Amusing choice of words," intoned their projected host, "and apropos. The task I ask in return is the destruction of the fastest man alive, the death of the hero known as . . . the Flash."

The assembled crooks were startled. They were thieves and con men, second-story men in bright outfits and masks; they weren't killers. For most of them, merely badgering one of the world's too-numerous heroes to distraction was rewarding enough.

"We're not hit men."

The words came from a gruff man with mirrored sunglasses. He had the look of one unaccustomed to deference, and this odd transaction was wearing on his nerves.

All but one of the others murmured their agreement. The dim house lights suddenly winked out, casting the auditorium into darkness. The image on the screen began to fade.

"Go, then! I will find someone else upon whom to bestow my largesse. . . ."

Out of the darkness one voice spoke.

"No, wait, I'll take the deal. I have no love for that dashing doofus," said a low, husky voice, growing bolder as it continued, "and I can use those weapons for a job I've got coming up."

The deep voice boomed again in the darkness, seeming to wash over the men. They were all anxious to be anywhere else.

"Stay. The others, get out. Forget you were here."

The blond man was on his feet, making his way to an exit. "I'm so gone, I'm already putting the key in my front door."

Seven departed quickly.

One stayed to listen.

"Here is what you will do . . . ," the voice in the dark began.

CHAPTER 1

The sign arching over the twelve-foot security gate read METACON TECHNOLOGIES—RESEARCH AND DEVELOPMENT DIVISION. The smaller but more urgent sign below read HIGH-SECURITY FACILITY. ABSOLUTELY NO UNAUTHORIZED PERSONNEL ALLOWED BEYOND THIS POINT. The gate itself was missing.

It lay twisted, charred, and still smoking fourteen feet inside the security entrance. Something very forceful and very hot had ripped the heavy steel gate from its place and tossed it aside as though it were crumpled paper. A few yards beyond it lay the shattered remains of the guard station. Some very powerful unauthorized personnel had ignored the strongly worded prohibition against entry.

A sudden breeze stirred the night air as a faint crimson blur blew through the ruined gate. As the two dazed but unhurt guards pulled themselves from the wreckage of their shed, they found a tall, impressive young man staring curiously down at them. The guards could only return his stare. The young man was clad head to foot in crimson and gold, including the red mask that covered half his face.

"Flash?" said the older of the two guards.

"Some costumed jerk and his crew blasted their way inside!" the second guard blurted out.

The fastest human being on Earth, the Flash lived for constant motion. Standing still even for a moment was his idea of torture, his body twitching and vibrating too fast for the human eye to see, in anticipation of renewed action. But now the speedster tried, as he always did, to contain his desire and forced himself to listen for a seeming eternity to the guards' story. It confirmed everything he had already learned from the Justice League alert.

"Unless I very much miss my guess," said Flash, "the rest of the Justice League has already got this creep well in hand." He nodded at the sound of approaching sirens. "Police are on their way too. Stay put, you might need medical attention."

With that, the Scarlet Speedster made for the main complex, moving so fast he appeared to be no more than a fading scarlet streak.

"Can't leave all the fun to the others . . . ," mused Flash with a wide, brash smile.

Elsewhere on the wooded and pleasant Metacon grounds stood the main research and development building, shaken now by strange internal tumult. Through the windows an impossible sight could be glimpsed: a powerful thunderstorm raging inexplicably within the lobby. Gale-force wind roared and bolts of lightning blazed as dense sheets of water poured from dark clouds scudding along the ceiling. The winged woman and the big man in green and black were being tossed madly by this bizarrely dislocated weather event.

Inside the building!

Green Lantern skidded on his back across the sopping carpet, sending up a splattering spray as he went. He held an arm across his eyes as yet another lightning bolt shot in his direction. On his finger he wore the famous ring that gave him his name and the power to make his will manifest. In the chaotic uproar, he couldn't focus enough will to use the ring as a flashlight.

Worse, he had lost track of his enemy in this ridiculous indoor hurricane. He didn't know where his partner, Hawkgirl, was either.

The two Justice Leaguers had been the first to respond to the Metacon alarm. They had entered, expecting to make short work of whatever criminal genius had been stupid enough to break into a facility on the Justice League's watch.

Just before the typhoon had swept in—from the cafeteria, Green Lantern was certain—he had glimpsed a clown in bright green. A clown brandishing what looked like a magic wand.

Then the clown waved that wand and all hell had broken loose, right in Green Lantern's startled face.

Too late, the Emerald Crusader had realized who they faced: a man who could summon and control the most powerful natural forces on earth. The Weather Wizard!

"Where's Flash?" wondered Green Lantern for at least the fifteenth time since the storm began.

Hawkgirl fell heavily onto the tumbled lobby furniture as hailstones the size of lightbulbs pelted her. Though she had protectively wrapped herself in her large wings, she felt every jolt of her fall. The smashing ice clods made themselves painfully evident as well. How had the Weather Wizard gained the upper hand so quickly?

A deafening explosion of thunder boomed in the confined space, followed quickly by sizzling blue-white spears of lightning. One bolt hit the overstuffed chair a few feet to Hawkgirl's left, blasting it to smoldering, blackened bits. Unable to get her bearings, she knew she could not long survive this blazing assault.

Abruptly, the lashing rain and wind seemed to abate. Hawkgirl looked out to find herself safely inside a large translucent bubble of bright emerald light energy. Green Lantern stood nearby, the glowing green enclosure emanating from his amazing ring. The next lightning strike bounced harmlessly off the barrier.

"We have to get to the lab," Green Lantern shouted over the storm's din, "before Weather Wizard succeeds in looting the place!"

"Where's Flash?" Hawkgirl shouted in response.

On several workstations under the high, arched ceiling of the vast laboratory space, impressive pieces of advanced technology sat in various stages of completion. In the center of the huge room stood a very tall, chrome-plated, tubular device on a pivoting stand. Every streamlined inch screamed *weapon of mass destruction!* This was the Ion Cannon, Metacon's current pride and joy. Weather Wizard and his four-member crew were gathered around this gleaming, towering marvel.

"Imagine the weather havoc I can wreak with the power of this bad boy blasting the clouds," the Weather Wizard whispered in awe.

"And thanks to the enhanced weapons we have," said the black-clad woman at the Wizard's side, "not even the high and mighty Justice League can stop us."

"Indeed, Tempest, indeed," chuckled the Weather Wizard.

"Now while we're here, let's see what other plunder we can grab."

From the vantage point of the high catwalk, the five criminals below looked like insects.

"They're bugs up close too," mused the Flash.

A microsecond later, Flash was no more than a hazy red streak heading straight down the wall to the main floor. The time had come, the speedster knew, for his fun to begin. Anything moving at human speed might as well have been frozen to Flash's speed-enhanced perception.

The large man in the black jumpsuit stood absolutely still, a wrench in his beefy hand. He was preparing to release the locking bolt from a small electromagnetic generator.

Another henchman was frozen in the act of grabbing greedily at a pair of oversized electron pistols.

The woman known as Tempest was about to snatch up a stack of top-secret files.

A short, stocky thug stood with a hammer raised above the cabinet lock he was about to smash.

The Weather Wizard grinned like a demented statue stroking the gleaming shell of the Ion Cannon.

To the Flash, they were all like frozen fish in a very small barrel.

A crimson wind swept through the room. The large man suddenly smashed himself in the head with his wrench. His howls of pain and confusion still rang in the air as the pistol-wielding thief clawed the empty air where his prizes had lain an instant before. At that exact moment, Tempest was lost in a flurry of documents. The vandal with the hammer stumbled backward; his trousers suddenly puddled around his ankles. The Weather Wizard's head slammed into the side of the Ion Cannon with a resounding *bong*. Flash strobed to a stop, contentedly holding the Wizard's wand.

A full eighth of a second had elapsed. Why rush when you're having a good time?

The lab doors were pushed open by a large emerald battering ram. Immediately, Green Lantern and Hawkgirl entered, both itching for battle. Lowering her heavy mace, Hawkgirl sighed to see the criminals reduced to five stunned heaps on the lab floor. Flash was leaning with too-studied relaxation against the Ion Cannon. He feigned a yawn as he idly snapped the wand in two.

"What took you guys so long?" the speedster asked with a grin.

"*We* were caught in the storm trap the Wizard set

for those of us who showed up first, glory boy," Green Lantern said. "We could have used your help."

"Hey, you *had* it, G.L.," Flash protested, smiling. "I was in here wrapping up the climatic creeps."

"Are we going to have this conversation again? You've got to start taking this work more seriously, Flash," said Hawkgirl with a sigh.

"Why work that hard when my speed keeps me miles ahead of jerks like this?"

The Weather Wizard had carefully pulled himself to his feet. In his hand was a small but lethal-looking silver pistol he had pulled from his wide belt. The pistol was aimed at Flash, who hadn't yet deigned to notice.

Flash whirled at the sound of the pistol's trigger. Incredibly, the fastest man alive was too late—the intensely bright bolt of crackling blue energy was already smashing into his chest.

For the first time in his speedy career, the Flash ran out of luck.

CHAPTER 2

Flash staggered back more in surprise than anything else as the bolt struck his white-and-gold lightning chest emblem dead center. The blue-white energy crawled swiftly across his torso, sizzling like a barbecued steak. The light show was startling, but the feeling . . .

"It . . . tickles . . . ?" said the chuckling speedster.

The energy dissipated as quickly as it had appeared. Flash stood wide-eyed and grinning but obviously no worse for the experience. Baffled, the Weather Wizard desperately attempted to fire the tiny pistol again and again but got only hollow, rasping clicks for his efforts. Whatever the weapon was, it was empty now.

"That . . . that was *supposed* to destroy you forever," groaned the Wizard. "What a gyp."

"I'd get my money back if I were you," said Flash as he cocked his arm. "Hope you saved your Thugs 'R' Us receipt."

Flash's crimson fist whooshed forward, delivering a thousand-mile-an-hour punch to the Weather Wizard's jaw. The dazed villain hopped backward several feet before sliding bonelessly to the floor.

"I don't suppose I should mention that he'd never have gotten off that shot if you'd been paying attention, Flash," said a weary Green Lantern.

"He could have fried you, Flash," added Hawkgirl with concern.

"I didn't know you cared, bird lady," mocked Flash. He jokingly flexed his right bicep in an exaggerated display of vigor. "But I'm fine, guys. His little popgun was a joke, and I got the job done with time to spare. All that exertion did make me hungry, though." Flash smiled crookedly. "Who's up for six or eight Big Bang breakfasts at Carmine's?"

"Is food all you think about?" said Green Lantern.

"I burn a lot of fuel moving as fast as I do, G.L.," said Flash with the same guileless grin. "And it's time to fill the ol' tank."

Green Lantern turned away and willed himself to stay calm. He knew by now that the speedster's attention span moved faster than his feet. Trying to inspire responsibility in Flash was like trying to teach a poodle to speak French.

"You go on, Flash, we'll wrap up here," said Hawkgirl, her large wings giving dramatic emphasis to her resigned shrug. Flash, of course, was long gone before she'd finished speaking.

Flash breezed out through the front gate, past the gathered police, fire, and emergency vehicles and personnel. With the situation in good hands, Flash moved on into the night, exulting in the feel of the wind against his face. As always, he enjoyed the way the streetlights elongated into bright and colorful banners, the way the night's many sounds made a strange and wonderful music. Speed was a full sensory joy for Flash, and he never took it for granted. His power was a gift, and he treasured it.

He knew Green Lantern was right. He *should* act in a more mature fashion when it came to the use of his power and his responsibility to the world as a Justice Leaguer. What Green Lantern didn't understand was that the very power that made Flash everything he was made it difficult for him to be grounded. No one could understand how the speed made Flash feel, even when he was standing still.

Ever since the one-in-a-trillion accident that had bathed Wally West in the electrified chemicals that somehow gave him his superspeed, his very reality had changed. Now his blood surged through his body like liquid lightning. His every molecule hummed with surging, blazing, exploding power; his nerves sang with potential energy. Constantly. And Flash loved it.

Far from distracted, Flash was always focused ten steps ahead of everyone else. On the next excitement, the next battle, and yes, sometimes, the next meal.

There was no adequate way for the Flash to explain to anyone how amazing it felt to blaze through life at a blur. It was freedom; it was magic. When you were as fast as Flash, you could outrace everything . . . including your own problems.

Easing into a curve as he headed back toward the city, Flash accelerated effortlessly toward Mach 10. He moved faster and faster, enjoying every second of his rocketing progress.

Suddenly, something was very, very wrong. Flash

sensed the involuntary loss of velocity, the inexplicable hitch in his smooth muscular rhythms. His legs were beginning to feel heavy, his body leaden. Looking down at his chest, Flash was alarmed to see that the crawling, blue-white energy from the Weather Wizard's weapon had returned. He had less than a millisecond to consider this impossible sight. Less time than that to wonder what was going on . . .

. . . before the roaring, burning, blasting pain ripped through every cell of his body! Flash screamed in agony as he lost control and tumbled forward into the headlong rush of his momentum.

Flash skidded and rolled for a half mile down the empty roadway before crashing into a muddy ditch. The fallen speedster lay sprawled in a brackish puddle, his limbs still twitching and steaming. He was barely able to note how good the cool water felt against his abraded skin. Then unconsciousness overtook him.

Wally West awoke painfully, unable to open his crusted, burning eyes. Where was he? Had it been minutes or years since he had cannonballed down the highway on his back?

But more importantly, why had his speed so betrayed him? A bloodred haze of pain was his only answer as it lowered over his awareness like a heavy curtain. Flash dropped into sleep again, moaning in remembrance of the blue-white lightning and the nightmare agony it brought.

Green Lantern looked down at his badly injured friend, sorry suddenly to have shared only harsh words with the speedster earlier. The Emerald Crusader flew resolutely skyward, carrying his unconscious teammate gently within a glowing green capsule of energy from his ring. The Justice League's Watchtower headquarters had fantastic medical facilties. Green Lantern hoped he could get Flash there in time.

The huge, imposing satellite floated in silent vigil against the cold blackness of space. The Watchtower, the Justice League's orbiting headquarters, kept constant watch over the massive azure orb of the Earth gleaming beautifully below.

Inside, within the super advanced technology of the satellite's medical bay, the heavily bandaged Flash slept fitfully in the cocoon of a steel treatment pod. The jade giant in the flowing blue cloak hovered close, studying the electronic displays built into the pod.

The man's visage was not quite human, but his compassion and concern for the friend before him was easily recognizable. J'onn J'onzz, the hero known as the Martian Manhunter, winced slightly as he pondered Flash's vital signs.

"What do you think, J'onn?" asked the pacing Green Lantern. Hawkgirl stood by, looking grim.

The Manhunter's voice rumbled deeply, sadly. "The energy the Weather Wizard fired at him has woven itself into Flash's cellular matrix, I'm afraid."

"What does that mean?" asked Hawkgirl with concern.

"It means that the strange energy has a stranglehold on Wally's unique metabolism. The faster he moves, the tighter its grip on him," said J'onn slowly. "At rest, his body won't feel a thing . . ."

"But if he speeds . . . ?" Green Lantern said, dreading the answer he knew he would get.

"It may well crush the life from him," J'onn J'onzz croaked huskily.

Superman and Batman moved side by side into the infirmary, drawing stares as always even from their peers. Alone, each was extraordinary and striking; together, they were awe-inspiring. They were almost diametric opposites, but they were the strongest of allies no matter their differences.

The Man of Steel and the Dark Knight were the living embodiments of the ideals the League was sworn to uphold. They moved quickly into the room, joining the other heroes huddled around their injured comrade. Flash's condition was displayed on the screens, and everyone's silent attention was riveted to the images there.

Superman studied the image representing Flash's neural pathways. Blue lightning energy pulsed as it twisted and spread like a rampant weed through the speedster's system. The Man of Steel looked away, his expression one of empathetic pain.

"There has to be . . . something we can do," he whispered. "We can't just let him suffer."

"If I understand J'onn's diagnosis, Flash isn't in any pain, aside from his injuries—and the equipment is doing everything possible to ease that," said Batman.

Green Lantern spoke softly. "He's going to be in a

whole world of psychological pain once he realizes he can never run again."

Batman began striding toward the door, his cape flowing behind him like wings. All business, as always, the Dark Knight moved with purpose.

"We need to find out the source of that energy, Lantern," Batman said. "Let's you and I see where the Weather Wizard got that ray pistol."

As Batman and Green Lantern left, Hawkgirl and Superman watched them.

"His emotion just chokes you up, doesn't it?" asked Hawkgirl sarcastically.

"Brisk efficiency *is* an emotion for Batman—it's how he shows concern." Superman smiled slightly. "He cares, and he will get the answers."

In the steel cocoon of the medical equipment, Flash slept.

CHAPTER 3

The huge spotlights shot their glaring beams skyward in sweeping arcs above the massive, blocky building of the maximum-security facility. Stonegate Prison had a well-deserved reputation for being inescapable; no one got out—and no one got in, unless they belonged there.

Stripped of his gaudy green "work clothes" and his wand, the Weather Wizard was not at all impressive. A sturdy, brooding man with close-cropped dark hair, Mark Mardon huddled disconsolately on the hard bench in his cell. The rumpled orange prison-issue jumpsuit was hardly the garb of a master villain, he thought with disgust. As always, indignity dogged him. Maybe it was time to rethink his chosen occupation.

But thievery was the only work he'd ever known. From the days of his misspent youth, Mardon had followed the crooked road. Even before coming into his weather-controlling power, he had made a name for himself as a jewel thief. In fact, it was while running from the law that Mardon had made the discovery that changed his life.

Or rather, his brother had made the discovery. Unlike his younger sibling, Dr. Matthew Mardon had made better than good. A research scientist with a specialty in particle physics, Matthew had applied his efforts to research and discovery. The day Mark sought out his big brother for help hiding from the authorities, Matthew had refused him outright. He and the rest of the Mardon family had long ago given up on their black sheep.

Matthew had been distracted, though, anxious to get back to work on some project. Appealing to his brother's vanity and stalling for time, Mark had asked him what he was working on. Mark knew that Matt couldn't resist a bit of showing off.

The object Mark had soon come to think of as his weather wand was in a stand on the main worktable. Matt held it up and explained it to Mark. Firing specifically charged particles into the air, the wand could affect the atmosphere on a localized basis, causing weather phenomena in small, controlled bursts.

With a wave of the wand, fluffy flakes of snow fell impossibly out of nowhere to drift onto Mark's shoulders. He was amazed—what the heck *was* this thing? And how could he use it to his own profit?

Matthew Mardon had developed the wand as a miniature prototype of a larger device he hoped to construct. That device would be able to control the climate of entire cities, Matt gushed. Once he figured out how to enlarge the prototype, the sky was the limit.

It could be a boon to agriculture. It might be the end of hunger. It had the potential to change the world's economy. So far, however, Matthew Mardon hadn't found a way to make the device work on a larger scale. In the meantime, the wand was an interesting, if limited, model.

Mark Mardon had listened without really hearing. From his point of view, the wand was far from limited. He was already envisioning many uses for it, most of them illegal, immoral, and profitable.

His brother had rambled on about the scientific principles, but Mark had long since tuned him out, so total was his focus on this new prize. Besides, science wasn't his thing; the wand might as well have been magic. All Mark cared about was that the wand was the answer to a small-timer's prayers—and he had to have it.

Mark stopped pretending to be interested in his brother's lecture and waved him brusquely to silence. He demanded the wand. Matt instinctively understood that his nefarious brother had nothing but criminal designs on his weather technology. He refused, but Mark had already grabbed the wand and pointed it at the air above his scientist brother's head.

Later, he told himself that he hadn't really meant to harm Matt. The fact remained, however, that Mark had turned the wand against Matt and left him for dead. If it hadn't been for the timely interference of some rotten super heroes, Mark reflected, Matt would have died.

The wand was his, though, and from that moment on, Mark Mardon became the masked menace known as the Weather Wizard.

To no one's surprise, bank managers and jewelry store owners cooperated very quickly when confronted with indoor lightning storms. The Weather

Wizard became all Mark Mardon had ever dreamed of being. He was a celebrity criminal. He was rich and feared. He was a super villain.

Unfortunately, as Mardon had already discovered, super villains draw the attention of super heroes, and his own bad luck soon placed the Flash and other Justice Leaguers regularly on his rain-soaked trail. Superpowers trump even miniature hurricanes every time. The day Flash and the others had entered the Weather Wizard's life, the climate had grown steadily gloomier for Mark Mardon.

Sitting in his cell, Mardon kept going over and over his latest failure. The voice at the theater had promised him great things. Their deal was supposed to reverse all his Flash-centric bad luck. It was supposed to put him back on top. It was supposed to finish off the fast-footed creep for good!

But the gun had backfired—or fizzled, or whatever. It had failed. And once again Mardon was left wearing garish orange and looking at the world he was meant to conquer through a narrow slit in solid concrete.

"Nuts," said the hapless crook.

Suddenly, the dim grayness of Mardon's surroundings took on a brighter, greener cast. He looked up in amazement to see an emerald glow spreading in an oval pattern on the outer wall of his cell. Then the jade light seemed to take on a three-dimensional shape, like a bubble, which began swelling as if passing *through* the blank concrete wall. This had to be bad, Mardon thought.

Two figures began to appear within that growing emerald capsule, as if stepping phantom-like through the solid wall. Mardon shut his eyes and shook his head. This had to be a hallucination. Even with his rotten luck, he refused to believe in ghosts.

As the figures grew more solid, Mardon found himself wishing he did believe in haunts. That would have been preferable to facing Batman and Green Lantern while he was unarmed and incarcerated. Green Lantern's emerald ring power faded once it had transported the two fierce-looking heroes into Mardon's startled presence.

"Hey, you guys can't be in here without my lawyer being present," complained Mardon.

"That might be true," said Green Lantern. "If we were here about you."

"Tell us who gave you the weapons you used on the Metacon job, Mardon," the Dark Knight commanded.

"Especially the gun you shot at Flash," added Green Lantern.

Mardon looked very confused. Why did they care about that harmless piece of junk? He thought about trying to play it cool and tough, of stalling until he could figure the angle. But one look at the dark intensity of Batman's glowering stare dissolved all Mardon's courage.

"I—" Mardon's throat went suddenly dry, "I don't know who he was! He never showed himself, he didn't give his name. I swear, I have no idea who he was!"

"We're supposed to believe that this total stranger decided to give you high-tech weapons out of the goodness of his heart?" asked Green Lantern.

"From the sound of his voice, I don't know that he has a heart, Lantern," said Mardon. "All I know is he promised me that stuff in exchange for shooting the speedster with that popgun."

"And you don't know how the pistol works?" asked Batman as he hovered menacingly over the cowering prisoner.

"It *doesn't* work. Ask your Justice League buddies. It gave off a harmless flash of light and then . . . nothing," Mardon complained.

Green Lantern and Batman looked meaningfully at one another. Mardon watched and wondered, an idea growing in his devious criminal mind. Had the gun had a delayed effect? Had Flash dropped dead later on? Had he, Mark Mardon, become the man who brought down a super hero?

Mardon smiled slightly to himself as he calculated the prestige this would bring him among the others of his ilk. He was the guy who had done in the Flash. . . . Things were going to be different.

"What's this all about? Is Flash dead?" Mardon asked with barely concealed excitement.

"No," said Batman, "and you'd better pray it doesn't come to that. You don't want to see me that angry."

"Umm, n-no," stammered Mardon, "I—I guess I don't."

But he was talking to an empty cell. The heroes were gone. Mardon looked out the narrow window at the night sky and wondered what was going on.

He shuddered at the idea of finding out from Batman. Better to survive in ignorance than to face that merciless guy ever again. As he slumped onto the bench, Mardon's thoughts turned to the Flash. Far from wishing him ill, Mardon knew that his own continued health might depend on the speedster's.

"Long may the Flash run," Mardon said, toasting the air with an empty hand. "Long may he run!"

Flash moved swiftly through the city at sunset. The sky was a glorious golden orange, and the tall steel-and-glass buildings were gilded in reflected color. The city was bustling, people hurrying on their way as auto traffic swept through the streets in a smooth, swift flow.

Amidst this symphony of motion, Flash, of course, set the tempo. He raced in joy, the warm evening breeze washing over him like a welcoming stream. Speed was his means of expression, his vocabulary, and everything he ever wanted to say.

As always, it was glorious—

—until the speedster was suddenly jolted violently from his smooth forward momentum. Flash stumbled and skidded clumsily, losing his balance. He flailed his arms. Something was holding him back.

Flash looked down at his legs with horror. A giant human hand had somehow formed from the tarry black surface of the roadway. Impossibly, that as-phalt appendage clung tightly to his ankle, pulling him back and down. Flash grunted in surprise and disgust, struggling to surge forward out of the thing's grasp.

The hand held tightly, and try as he might, Flash could not break free. As he looked down and back, another hand was molding itself from the pavement, stretching out to grab his other leg. Flash called out in alarm, but the passing citizens could not or would not hear him.

Now three more huge hands morphed from the shiny black pavement, attached to arms elongating to reach and clutch at the speedster's scarlet uniform.

Unable to move, Flash felt helpless, lost. He was pulled backward and fell to the pavement, even as rushing traffic swept by without noticing.

Monstrous black hands clawed at Flash's throat, his limbs, his entire body, drawing him ever downward. All the hero could think of was that he needed to run, to get away—that was his only hope.

That hope died screaming. Flash was held tightly, pulled powerfully down and down, until he saw with wild revulsion that the street had become a bubbling, rippling liquid mass. The Flash was being swallowed into the sticky fluid, and there was nothing he could do about it.

He opened his mouth to scream, only to let jets of black goo rush in to fill his throat. Choking, Flash found himself at last below the surface. He was drowning in the middle of his city and he couldn't run, he couldn't escape, he couldn't even move.

Completely engulfed in thick, grasping darkness, Flash fell forever.

CHAPTER 4

Flash woke up in a bed in the infirmary of the Justice League Watchtower. Squinting against the glaring light, the speedster looked down at his bandaged, pain-racked body. He groaned more in frustration than suffering.

The accident hadn't been a nightmare after all. Though he'd been unconscious most of the time, Flash fully understood what had happened to him. In fact, he could feel the constricting hold of the energy that crawled like an unstoppable invading army through his cells. He sat up, wincing as his injuries made themselves known.

Despite the strange power inhibiting his physical movement, his metabolism still functioned at its normal accelerated rate. Flash's body was already nearly healed, but his spirit remained downcast. He limped to the large view port in the outer bulkhead wall of the infirmary. From this vantage, the earth was a blue gem against the velvet black of space.

Flash stared glumly down on his home planet. He held up his hand, as if cradling the tiny globe in his fingers. There was a time when the world had been no bigger than this to him, when there hadn't been one corner of the entire planet he couldn't race to in mere moments. Those days were long over now.

Flash turned from the view unmoved. Consumed by his own great loss, Flash wasn't in the mood to notice anything—including the strikingly beautiful visitor at the infirmary door.

"You're finally awake. Good," said Wonder Woman. "We've been worried for days."

Flash looked up to see the powerful Amazon Princess smiling at him with interest. Her strong, shapely, red-gold-and-blue-clad form would normally have elicited some leering remark from the Flash. But neither his heart nor his head was in it. He just couldn't bring himself to flirt, not even with such a regal beauty.

"If you're going to forgo clumsy attempts at flirtation,

I *am* worried." Wonder Woman smiled with gentle amusement.

"If you'll take a rain check, Diana, I can try to get back to you." He gave her a small, pained smile.

Flash turned away and limped slowly back to the bed. The low set of his shoulders spoke loudly of his mood. Wonder Woman watched him with sympathy, wishing there was something she could do or say to help her friend.

"Running fast is what I do. It's what makes me a Justice Leaguer," said Flash quietly.

"It's not *who* you are, though," said the Amazon Princess. "It's not what makes you a hero."

Flash could only stare at her. It was hard to know what to say; he wanted to believe her, but he couldn't.

"Your power is simply *how* you help people; the desire and drive to do so come from within you," said Wonder Woman.

"You take great pains to keep anyone from seeing how much you care, Flash, but you don't fool me. I know you have a hero's heart."

Flash grimaced. "A lot of good it'll do me if I can't move fast enough to get the job done."

"If your speed is gone, that's tragic, but it's not the end of the world. You'll find other ways to do what's needed." Wonder Woman placed a comforting hand on Flash's slumped shoulder.

"Yeah, I have so many other talents . . . ," mumbled the Flash.

"Don't be so down on yourself," chided Wonder Woman. "You'll always have a place with the Justice League."

"Right," said Flash. "I can always be the team mascot."

"Maybe we can get you a new costume with a big cartoon head."

Despite his mood, the Flash had to smile, both at the image and at the fact that the usually serious Wonder Woman had made the joke. Maybe he was taking all of this too seriously. As Wonder Woman had said, even if his power was gone forever, it wasn't the end of the world. He could still . . .

No, it *was* the end of the world for him. Who'd want a slow-moving super hero? His career as the Flash was over; it was massive denial to pretend otherwise. He had to tough it out and be realistic, however grim reality was.

But not right then. It was important to Diana that he stay optimistic. For her and his other friends, Wally resolved to put on his brave face.

"As of this moment," said Flash, "everyone has to stop feeling sorry for me. Especially me."

"It's a deal," said Wonder Woman.

The Martian Manhunter moved swiftly toward the communication console in the League's meeting room. The flashing alert signal indicated an incoming distress call.

"You've reached the Justice League Watchtower," said the Manhunter in his sonorous tone. "J'onn J'onzz here."

Suddenly the screen filled with electronic snow. Loudly hissing static blasted from the speakers. J'onn stepped back in surprise. Then, amid the crackling disturbance, there appeared the face of what seemed to be a great ape. And he was speaking.

This alarming image did not surprise the stoic Manhunter, however. He recognized Solovar, leader of a race of super-advanced intelligent apes.

Deep within the jungles of central Africa, the apes lived in quiet harmony within the confines of their futuristic citadel. The very few outsiders who knew of the place had dubbed it Gorilla City. A haven for scientific research and philosophical contemplation, the citizens of Gorilla City were peaceful and cooperative. Most of them.

"Thank goodness I have reached you! It . . . is Grodd. . . ," crackled the distorted voice from the communicator. "He has escaped!"

Without really thinking, J'onn thumbed a toggle switch on the console. A silent alert went out, summoning the Leaguers onboard to the meeting room.

The broadcast image of the wise gorilla leader flickered on screen, seeming to struggle against a storm of interference. Static ebbed and surged, drowning out whatever Solovar said next.

"—empting to usurp control . . . Gorilla City!" The ape leader's message barely came through.

J'onn's dark eyes widened. Grodd was the lone malevolent gorilla of his incredible race, a scheming renegade every bit as advanced as his fellows. Superscience was the ape's weapon in his ongoing quest for world domination.

As Grodd considered himself the smartest creature on earth, he saw no reason why he should not be made unquestioned leader over all of creation. The huge and hairy rogue reserved his greatest enmity for humanity. The Justice League had clashed several times with this malicious primate. Their victories had never been easy.

"What is it, J'onn?" said Superman as he moved swiftly into the room. Green Lantern, Hawkgirl, Wonder Woman, and Batman followed, all looking at the communicator screen. Flash entered last, limping painfully.

"A distress call from Solovar of Gorilla City," said the Martian hero. "It appears that Gorilla Grodd is once again on the loose."

On the screen, the distorted image cleared again momentarily. Solovar, looking more concerned, implored the Leaguers: ". . . is intent on taking over our citadel! . . . need the Justice League's immediate assistance!"

The assembled heroes looked with grave concern at the screen, even as Solovar's visage was replaced by flashing, roaring static. The connection had been severed; he did not reappear.

There was no conversation. The Leaguers all knew what had to be done.

"We'll leave immediately," said Superman simply.

"Can I catch a ride with one of you?" asked Flash.

"You can't go on this one, Flash. You're still healing," said Green Lantern.

"Yes," said Batman. "Stay and recuperate. We'll
handle this."

"It won't be easy without you, of course."
Superman added, "but we'll do the best we can."

Flash's answering smile did not reach his eyes. He
recognized that this was his new lot in life. He was
now the guy they protected. The guy they patronized.

"Okay, then," he said, "send me a postcard."

Flash dropped heavily into the chair at the communication console. He pressed a control and leaned
back. On the screen, the image of the departing
Justice Leaguers was replaced by a picture of a row
of athletic young women in track uniforms. They
stood on a carefully lined track, waiting to begin a
race.

"People running. Perfect," moaned Flash. "Maybe
the sports channel isn't the way to go."

Wally's thumb hit the button on the remote. The
screen began flipping past image after image. Wally
paused on an old black-and-white television pro-
gram. A comically wild-eyed comedian in khakis and

a pith helmet was flailing and shouting as he sank past his waist in fake quicksand. The cheap plastic jungle behind him shook faintly from his exertions. Canned laughter roared.

"What's so funny about that?" said Flash with a sour expression.

He pushed the remote again.

CHAPTER 5

Batman, Hawkgirl, the Martian Manhunter, and Wonder Woman were protected from the rigors of traveling through the earth's atmosphere by a bubble of Green Lantern's ring energy. Superman, powerful enough to handle reentry on his own, flew alongside.

They landed on a dirt road in the middle of a dense, green African jungle. The entrance to Gorilla City was not far away.

"We'll split up and go in separately," said Superman. "Until we figure out exactly what's happening, we'll stay hidden."

"Yes, no need to show ourselves yet. The element of surprise may come in handy if Grodd has taken over," agreed Batman.

"Let's remember, people: that big ape can control minds," warned Green Lantern.

Wonder Woman nodded. "We only beat him last time because . . . because Flash could move even faster than Grodd's thoughts."

"Then we will need to rely on strategy and stealth," concluded the Manhunter.

The heroes moved off, each seeking his own path.

Superman moved silently through the dense foliage. The Man of Steel glided along, his red-booted feet just inches off the ground. All around him were the sounds of indigenous life: the call of birds, the chatter of small animals, the grunts of larger predators foraging in the nearby weeds. Even Superman's hypersensitive hearing could detect no more threatening sound.

About half a mile ahead, Superman knew, lay the invisible barrier that marked the perimeter of Gorilla City. He would go that far and then carefully scout along the edge for any sign of trouble. So far, however, everything seemed calm.

It was nothing loud or dramatic that unsettled Superman in the next moments. Rather, it was the sudden cessation of the normal buzz of the jungle. Something had alerted the inhabitants, frightening them into frozen silence.

Superman used his enhanced vision to scan the area around him. He saw nothing. He strained to listen more carefully. He heard nothing. But he knew without a doubt that something was coming for him.

He reached for the Justice League communicator he wore in his ear. He needed to send a warning to his fellow heroes, but even Superman was not fast enough to complete that action. Out of the corner of his eye, he saw a blurred shape rushing toward him at remarkable speed. Superman whirled, too late.

The huge brown gorilla swung out of nowhere and slammed feetfirst into Superman's broad chest. The hero was propelled backward like a missile. Tough and resilient as his Kryptonian body was, Superman felt every painful inch of his passage through the underbrush. He tried to focus on controlling his wild ride, and he might have succeeded had he not crashed hard the next second into the broad, heavy bole of a gum tree.

Merely winded when a normal man might have been crushed, Superman rose painfully to his feet and looked around. Again, the evidence of all his senses told him he was utterly alone. In an impossible instant, however, he was once again under attack by charging apes. This time three of them attacked, kicking, punching, butting into the Man of Steel with punishing force.

Superman attempted to fight back, but his thrashing fists met empty air. His simian assailants were moving too quickly even for someone of his great power.

Finally Superman's flashing fist connected with something satisfyingly solid. A grunt followed by a thunderous crash revealed his enemy—and the means of their incredible swiftness.

On the ground lay an unconscious ape warrior. He was strapped into some sort of propulsion device made of gleaming chrome tubing, fuel pods, and a tapered jet nozzle. Steam rose from the exhaust tube. In the ape's hand was a shock weapon in the shape of a streamlined baton. Superman took a second to marvel at the technology. Gorilla City was far ahead of the human world, but only a twisted mind like Grodd's would pervert that scientific genius to such lethal ends.

Superman ducked as another attacker zoomed at him. The flying gorilla made a 180-degree turn and

rocketed again at the Man of Steel. Superman braced
for the impact, trying to focus on his attacker, but the
sudden buzz of another assailant sounded behind
him.

An incredibly powerful blow to the head drove
Superman to his knees. Frustration and pain roiled
within him as he tried to gather all his strength to
strike back. Superman looked up at the sound of approaching feet. What he saw startled and confused
him even more than the zooming ape attackers.

Before him stood a chimpanzee with a large tubular device in his hands. The chimp smiled crookedly
at the hero.

"Say good night, Superman," the chimpanzee said
in a cheerful, high-pitched voice. He aimed the
tube—a weapon, obviously—at Superman and pulled
the trigger.

A flash of intense, blistering light filled the air for a
moment before Superman crashed hard to the
ground and lost consciousness.

The cave mouth gaped in the sandstone of the
rocky hillside. The cavern itself was big enough for a
tall man to move about easily. Green Lantern peered

intently into the darkness. In the inky blackness beyond the entrance, it was impossible to tell how deep the cave went into the hill.

The ground at the entrance was well trampled; many feet had passed that way, and recently. Green Lantern moved with caution into the dim coolness of the cavern. Perhaps this was the secret entrance to the apes' citadel; it might even be the gathering place for Grodd's rebellious cohorts.

Only the echoing sound of rushing water broke the silence. The tunnel sloped downward; the air grew cooler, damper. Ahead on the curving cavern wall the Emerald Crusader could see the shimmering golden reflection of light on water. The scent of river water filled the air.

Green Lantern found himself looking down on a natural grotto and a briskly running underground river. Churning and rippling, it flowed off through a narrow passage into the depths of the earth. The walls glowed with the soft yellow of natural phosphorescence, glinting off the burbling surface of the water and throwing antic reflections onto the rocks above. Green Lantern pondered his next move.

The next move was not his to make, however. Green Lantern did not notice the surface of the river begin to churn slightly. Something was rising quickly to its surface. In the weird flickering light, the thing emerging from the water looked even more nightmarish. It was a gorilla—a very wet gorilla—and it was wearing a sleek metal-and-glass breathing device over the lower portion of its grotesque face. Its eyes blazed a shimmering gold.

Two more soggy apes wearing similar equipment followed the first. They swam silently toward the shore behind the unsuspecting Green Lantern.

One ape slipped on the damp slope, a grating sound that echoed in loud warning. Immediately, the Galactic Guardian aimed his ring and projected an expanding shield of emerald power. The shield slammed into the nearest gorilla with the force of a speeding truck. It smashed the gorilla back into the river.

The apes unholstered handheld energy weapons and took aim at Green Lantern. A low, whining hum sounded in the echoing chamber.

Sizzling bolts of golden energy leapt from the strange weapons. Instinctively, Green Lantern ringed a barrier to protect himself from the blasts.

"Drop those FryDaddies, gentlemen, they're useless against my power ring!" said Green Lantern.

Twin bolts of energy sliced through the green shield like razor blades through paper. The Emerald Crusader was startled—his ring was supposed to protect him! He had less than a millisecond to ponder this impossibility before the bolts lanced into him and threw him backward.

Green Lantern bounced hard off the cavern wall and crumpled to the floor. All three gorilla thugs approached him cautiously, weapons drawn.

"Grodd was right," said one of the attackers. "The frequency of our golden energy short-circuits the ring's power!"

"Long enough to flatten the human scum, anyway," said another with a cruel chuckle. "Now come on, let's get him to Grodd."

Leaping up suddenly, Green Lantern fired a laser-like beam from his ring and blew a weapon from one ape's paw. He followed with a torrent of golf-ball-sized globes of green energy fired through the air at another foe.

The green spheres pelted the second ape attacker mercilessly, shattering his energy weapon in the process. A body slam from a green battering ram sent the third ape sailing back into the river.

That was probably too easy, thought the Emerald Crusader. *But it was fun.*

Green Lantern never saw the fourth, larger gorilla behind him. A huge charge of crackling golden energy ripping through his body was the only warning he received, and by that time, it was too late to act. Too late to do anything but slide helplessly into oblivion.

Her wings flexing powerfully, Hawkgirl swooped low over the trees. She scanned the jungle below for signs of Grodd and his rebel band but saw nothing. She carried her mace ready in her left hand.

Hawkgirl spiraled low over the grassy plain. There, a pride of lions hunted in the tall grass. A police officer on her home planet of Thanagar, Hawkgirl appreciated the sight—she too was an expert at stalking prey. But where was her current quarry?

Unbeknownst to the Thanagarian Fury, the prey she sought was near, but not below. Metallic wings beating the air, the huge simian thug flew rapidly through the air, intent on a hunt of his own. In his huge paw was a gleaming steel battle hammer.

They met in midair. Hawkgirl wasn't sure if it was

anything but pure instinct that made her turn to face him in that last instant. Her reaction was textbook reflex as her mace blurred in a wide arc to smash with a clang against the ape's hammer. The shuddering vibration ran up the Winged Warrior's powerful arms. The flying gorilla spun away clumsily like a loose kite.

"Haven't had those wings very long, eh?" chided Hawkgirl. "I was born with mine."

A pinioned predator, Hawkgirl swooped after her flailing enemy, her mace raised and ready. The flying combatants clashed again, and this time Hawkgirl's shattering weapon sent the battle hammer plummeting to the jungle floor.

On follow-through, Hawkgirl slammed the haft of her mace against the ape's jaw. He grunted in pain and surprise—and spun earthward. Hawkgirl watched him fall.

She suddenly swooped after him. A fall from this height would kill him, and she couldn't allow that to happen to even the worst enemy. She stretched out a hand to grab his ankle.

To her utter surprise, her quarry arrested his own fall and zoomed upward again, out of her reach.

Hawkgirl pumped her wings and swept up in an arc, her mace raised threateningly as she pursued him.

"You're unarmed, and I'm much better at this flying stuff then a lump like you will ever be. Give up, Hairy!"

But he wasn't completely unarmed. A scarlet beam shot out of his wrist gauntlet and slammed into Hawkgirl's shoulder. A blazing pain radiated through her body as a wave of crimson overtook her vision.

Hawkgirl fell to earth like a stone. Her enemy zeroed in to collect his prize.

CHAPTER
6

J'onn J'onzz was a telepath. All Martians were, though he was now the last of his kind. Martians also possessed complete control over their physical density, giving the Manhunter the incredible ability to become both invisible and intangible.

It was this latter capacity that made his passage through the jungle so easy. A pair of Grodd's gorilla soldiers patrolled the area, armed with high-tech rifles. J'onn followed them without being noticed and drifted closer to listen to the apes' conversation.

"Grodd will be pleased. The winged woman, the ring wearer, and the strong man have all been captured. Soon the Justice League will be his," said one ape guard.

The Manhunter listened with alarm. He'd have to warn the others immediately. He focused his mind on Batman first, picturing the Dark Knight clearly in his mind's eye. He beamed his urgent thoughts out into the ether, seeking contact with Batman's sharp mind.

The message never reached its intended target. Instead, J'onn's mind filled with cold darkness that washed back over him. He tried to disengage but could not; whatever he had contacted had a firm mental grip on his psyche.

The Manhunter started in terror as his mind filled with images of raging fire, his one weakness. The flames roared closer and closer; there was no escape. J'onn was a prisoner in his own mind.

The blaze consumed the Martian's awareness. It drove him deeper into his unconscious, seeking escape. His mind shut down in defense. His body dropped into the jungle brush, slowly becoming solid and visible once more. By that time, though, the gorilla soldiers had moved on. The Manhunter lay slumped in the weeds.

Five apes surrounded Wonder Woman. Each of them grinned maliciously and carried glowing energy whips. Mere moments before, they had dropped out of the trees to surprise her.

One of the beasts snapped his whip and it unfurled like an electric snake. Wonder Woman ducked under the lash. Dodging another flashing whip, she executed a springing somersault and launched herself feetfirst at one of the apes. Her scarlet boots smashed into the gorilla's face.

Wonder Woman's hand dropped to her belt, and she grabbed her Golden Lasso. The line flew unerringly at its target, wrapping around another ape's ankles. The Amazon yanked the glowing cord as she ran, upending the lassoed primate. Two more apes cracked their whips, but Wonder Woman was simply too fast to be caught.

Raised on the island of Themyscira among her Amazon sisters, Diana was trained from birth to be a perfect warrior. In battle, she came alive. Her speed and strength were incredible, her fighting skills unmatched.

Wonder Woman lashed a flying kick into another adversary's thick torso. The gorilla crashed hard into a tree and went down to stay. The Amazon Princess was still moving, targeting yet another opponent.

Wonder Woman leapt over another flashing energy

whip. She crashed her fists into another ape's face. In the confusion, Wonder Woman broke for the trees. She needed to alert her fellow Leaguers.

Unable to rouse any of the other heroes on the scene on her comm link, Wonder Woman put in a call to the Watchtower.

Flash dozed in the chair at the communication console. Healing was fatiguing work, and there wasn't much stimulation in doing nothing. The shrill electronic beep woke him roughly.

On the screen, Wonder Woman's beautiful face appeared. The jungle filled the background with green and brown. Flash was in no mood for banter, but the Amazon's intense expression would have discouraged that inclination anyway.

"I don't have much time, Flash. The distress call was a trap. Grodd was waiting for us!" Wonder Woman said.

"Sheesh . . . even Superman?" Flash asked incredulously.

"Yes. Grodd has armed his apes with advanced weaponry. Extremely powerful."

Flash sat back heavily, totally stunned. He had

never felt more useless; his friends were in danger and he was stuck in the Watchtower, literally powerless.

"Flash, I don't know how much longer I can evade them. We need your help now!" Wonder Woman said.

"I can't do anything," said Flash bitterly.

"Yes, you can. You're a hero no matter what. Take the *Javelin* and get here as soon—"

Wonder Woman never finished the sentence. An energy whip thrashed into her from behind, snaking itself around her shoulders. The whip crackled with blazing energy, and the Amazon screamed in agony.

Before the communicator shut down, Flash had a chance to see this dreadful sight in vivid, stomach-churning detail. He pushed himself up from the console and ran toward the hanger deck. With or without superspeed, he couldn't leave the Justice League in that murderous beast's clutches!

Batman crept carefully through the brush, looking intently ahead through the small binocular-like device in his hand. Through the special lenses, he could track the perimeter of Gorilla City's force field enclosure. Somewhere along this path, Batman had expected to find evidence of an access through the barrier, and at last, he found it.

Batman whirled at the sound of a snapping branch behind him. What he saw chilled even the stoic crimefighter. J'onn J'onzz staggered out of the jungle, obviously disoriented and in great pain. The Martian's green skin had taken on a chalky, grayish pallor, and his deep-set dark eyes were cloudy and unfocused. The Manhunter croaked out a strangled cry for help as he dropped heavily to the ground.

Batman moved quickly to his comrade's aid. Bending over his fallen friend, Batman checked J'onn's vital signs.

"Breathing is shallow and pulse is racing," muttered Batman. "Presumably that's bad even for a Martian."

Batman leaned closer, speaking softly but urgently to his friend.

"J'onn! What's happened? Who did this to you?"

"Grodd . . . in my head! Get him out of my head!" the Manhunter whispered hoarsely.

Batman had no idea what to make of this strange request. He knew that the Manhunter was a telepath, but even the Dark Knight couldn't help him in that realm. "Tell me what to do, J'onn," Batman urged.

The Martian Manhunter's slack expression and bleary gaze vanished immediately. Suddenly his eyes blazed with intelligence and his face took on a fierce aspect. The transformation was so abrupt it startled the unflappable Batman.

"J'onn, are you all right?" Batman said, "J'onn, speak to me!"

The Manhunter stood up in a fluid motion. He glowered down at the Dark Knight.

"J'onn is gone, Batman. There's no one here but us monkeys," said the Manhunter in a chilling singsong.

With that, the Martian smashed his massive jade fist into Batman's jaw with incredible speed and terrible force.

The Martian Manhunter slung Batman's unconscious form carelessly over his shoulder and walked stiffly into the jungle. As he walked, he laughed.

Anyone who heard that cold laughter might have thought it had come from the throat of Grodd himself.

CHAPTER
7

Like a gleaming steel blade the sleek *Javelin 7* sliced through Earth's atmosphere. At the controls of the League's space jet sat a pensive Flash. The automatic pilot was locked into a course for central Africa . . . and Gorilla City.

There was no question that he would attempt to rescue his captive friends; he had not hesitated for a second. But now that he had a few unoccupied moments, Flash began to wonder how he was supposed to pull it off. Without his superspeed, what could he do? He was just an ordinary man now, no longer a super hero.

His mind went back to what Wonder Woman had said. Despite all the amazing things they could do, those the world called super heroes were people first and super second. That was true even of the Martian Manhunter, who sometimes seemed to Wally more human than most people born on this planet. Maybe it was true of Flash himself as well.

Maybe.

He couldn't dismiss the wisdom of the Amazon's words. She was probably right, as usual. Still, while it might be true that he was far more than just his power, it was also true that his speed was what made Flash special. Deprived of his superswiftness, he was just Wally West, extremely ordinary guy.

Worse, without his power, his options numbered exactly zero. He'd go from matching wits with super crooks such as the Weather Wizard to asking people if they wanted fries with their burgers. Being Flash wasn't only everything Wally knew how to do, it was all he had ever dreamed of being. Without it, life looked like one endless road to boredom and frustration.

Reflection of this sort was alien to the former Fastest Man Alive. For him, thought was synonymous with action. Deep thought had never been his forte.

Wally West divided his life into two distinct periods:

the agonizing tedium before he was Flash, and the supersonic wonder ever since. Growing up in the bucolic American Midwest, he had had enough slowness and changelessness in eighteen years to last for twenty-six lifetimes.

From the window of his childhood bedroom, Wally could see across what seemed like a million miles of flat nothingness to the razor-sharp horizon line. If he chose to, he could watch the huge red thresher on its infinitely slow crawl down rows and rows of wheat ripe for harvest. He could also have chosen to watch paint dry on the barn.

School was more eternal torture, though most of the subjects had come easily to him. Life had lacked challenge in Blue Valley, and Wally learned early on that he desperately needed to be challenged.

When the accidental electrochemical dousing left him with his incredible speed, Wally knew that his days of smalltown boredom were over at last. Nothing would ever hold him back again. Life had been filled with challenge from that moment on.

Well, the Flash thought, rushing into action against the immensely powerful Gorilla Grodd without superspeed was as big a challenge as he had ever faced. Through the *Javelin 7*'s windshield, he could see the deep green of the African veldt approaching quickly. He wouldn't have much time to make a plan; he had to try and focus.

Batman had no powers, and Wally sometimes believed the Dark Knight to be the most effective hero he'd ever met. There wasn't a moment the great detective didn't anticipate; there wasn't a move he didn't have planned. Batman was always at least ten steps ahead of everyone else.

But Batman had trained from his youth to be the best a human could be. He hadn't blundered into power by sheer luck, as Wally had. Strategy was not Flash's specialty, but he'd have to learn. And—the irony wasn't lost on him—he'd have to learn it quickly.

He'd never had to take the time to learn anything. With his speed, Flash could adjust on the fly, improvising his solutions in the blink of an eye. That's why it always seemed to Green Lantern that Flash was sloppy and undisciplined. Of course, compared with Green Lantern, everyone was sloppy and undisciplined.

Next to Batman, Green Lantern was the most focused guy Wally knew. He was always the man with the plan, and he never deviated from it. It worked for

Green Lantern, Wally recognized, because he needed structure the way Wally needed freedom. Still, going into battle with Grodd, Wally knew he'd have to take a page from the Emerald Crusader's book too. He'd have to stay focused and disciplined, however strange that was to his character. It was the only way to survive.

He'd need stealth too. No longer capable of moving so fast as to seem invisible, Wally would need to exercise extreme caution and creativity in sneaking past Gorilla City's defenses. If only he had J'onn's abilities, Flash reflected, then he'd have no trouble getting in. While he couldn't become intangible or blend in with his surroundings as the Martian could, the Flash could learn much from the Manhunter's calm determination in approaching any problem. Rushing in would only get himself and the others killed.

Whatever came, he'd have to tough it out. Superman wouldn't be stopped by the loss of his powers. The Man of Steel was the most dedicated hero Wally knew. Even without his strength, his enduring spirit would drive him on. He'd be "super" even as a ninety-eight-pound weakling.

And you couldn't ask for a greater inspiration when it came to perseverance than Hawkgirl, Wally thought. Forced by circumstances to live far from her home world, she hadn't given up. She had adjusted and carried on her fight for justice in her new home. No one was tougher; no one more tenacious.

Wally knew he'd keep her strengths in mind as he headed into battle. He'd be lucky to manage a fraction of the greatness his fellow Leaguers represented.

The *Javelin 7* zoomed just over the tree line, circling for a landing.

"Well, it's show time . . . ," said the Flash, pulling his scarlet mask over face.

Gorilla City was a startlingly modern accumulation of gleaming high-tech buildings made of steel and glass. It couldn't have been more out of place in the surrounding jungle foliage. Fortunately, a force field shielded the city from view. Normally the city bustled with apes going about their daily business, but now it was empty and eerily quiet.

Inside the main dome, in the large council chamber, mighty Grodd held court. Even among the huge apes of his remarkable species, Grodd was startling in his massive size and power.

Around the room, row upon row of silent gorillas stood in dazed passivity. Thanks to Grodd's superior mental force, the entire citizenry was under his control. Even the great Solovar, beloved leader of all the superintelligent apes, was in his thrall. Only Grodd's true disciples moved about with free minds.

At the back of the room stood a huge, black steel box, a gleaming and ominous machine of some sort. Inside, the hum of the device's works droned incessantly, and sparks could be seen through a vent. A complex array of lit dials and gauges on the machine's face hinted at a tremendous amount of power harnessed to some malefic purpose. The thing throbbed and pulsed with mind-numbing energy.

In fact, this great and terrible engine was the source of Grodd's absolute authority; a device that amplified his already formidable mind control to a level that could turn even the mighty Justice League into docile pawns. Grodd had made himself a king, and this unwieldy generator was his scepter of office.

Secure in his unchallenged power, Grodd slumped indolently in the large makeshift throne in the center of the room. His dark, piercing eyes were studying the six helpless super heroes in front of him. The Leaguers were trapped like flies in amber, surrounded by an energy field that sapped their powers and damped their wills.

"This is greatly satisfying," rumbled Grodd. "In this reduced state, you fools are almost amusing."

Grodd lumbered down from his throne to stalk toward the heroes. He stood facing them boldly, defiantly. They were his to toy with as he pleased.

"You have all danced at my command, without even suspecting it. It was I who supplied that idiotic Weather Wizard with advanced weaponry. It was I who willed him to target the cretin Flash for his special punishment. Flash has always proved an especially difficult foe, dealing me defeat in the past. I do not suffer that well. Now . . . none of you will stand in my way."

Grodd smiled, a grotesque display of jagged, yellowed fangs. "Soon I will bring about my new world order, and all humans will rightly serve their ape masters forever!"

Grodd turned to behold his massive black generator, his enormous arms spread wide, as if encompassing the entire world.

"As I speak, my agents prepare to construct a network of these devices across the globe! Once they are activated, I will broadcast my will to every weak human mind on Earth . . . and I will be master of them all!"

Grodd marched away impatiently. His lackeys hovered, attempting to anticipate their leader's whims. None dared trigger the wrath of his awesome temper. Grodd turned on his heels and railed at the room.

"With the overrated Justice League in my total control, and the annoying insect Flash neutralized, no one can stop me!"

The great gray gorilla narrowed his glittering eyes and hissed out a triumphant pronouncement.

"Soon the entire earth will bow in absolute obeisance to almighty Grodd!"

Grodd sent a mental command to his helpless subjects. Like puppets, the dazed ape audience applauded with empty enthusiasm. Grodd looked around, basking in the acclaim he had demanded. But it wasn't enough. Something was missing.

Grodd smiled and focused his will on the trapped Justice League. Within the containment field, their forms twitched. Their hands rose as if they were mindless automatons. Grodd pressed on mercilessly.

Superman, Wonder Woman, Green Lantern, Batman, Hawkgirl, and the Martian Manhunter wore slack, dazed expressions. Their hearts and minds were elsewhere as they clapped their hands in forced applause.

Grodd dropped back into his throne, letting the coerced approbation wash over him. This was the treatment he deserved. This was the glory that was his birthright!

The sound of mechanical clapping went on and on, echoing coldly in the large room.

CHAPTER 8

Flash flipped the cloaking control switch on the *Javelin 7*'s console. The steel blue ship was surrounded for a second by a shimmering halo of light; then it seemed to vanish.

Flash stepped out of his now hidden transport, seeming to materialize in midair eight feet up, and clambered to the grassy plain. It was twilight, and the surrounding jungle was eerily silent. The speedster moved with equally quiet caution up a trampled path in the tall grass. According to the *Javelin*'s scanners, Gorilla City was a half mile to the west. Though he couldn't see it yet, he headed in that direction, keeping to the shadows.

The sound of heavy footsteps alerted Flash, and he

flattened against the trunk of a large nearby tree. Two heavily armed ape sentries walked toward him down the path, talking quietly. Flash waited, barely breathing. The apes lumbered past without noticing him.

After a beat, Flash stepped back onto the path and headed for Gorilla City. He hadn't gotten ten feet before he heard a croaking shout behind him.

"Halt, intruder! In the name of Grodd, stop!"

Flash risked a glance over his shoulder only to see the ape sentries running his way. One had his weird rifle pointed right at the stunned speedster.

The gun barked a low, guttural sound as it was fired. Flash could see a blazing projectile the size of a billiard ball zooming his way. He stepped aside just in time.

Behind Flash a tree exploded into flaming toothpicks. He dropped and rolled quickly into the underbrush. The apes ran closer, raising their rifles to the firing position.

Flash dodged and ran clumsily through the low growth. How ignominious for the Fastest Man Alive to be sprinting like an out-of-shape commuter running for a bus. The sounds of two more shots echoed in the damp night air. More explosions erupted right at the Flash's heels. At this rate, he was not going to get away.

Flash stumbled over unseen rocks; he grabbed at the bole of a tree for balance. Winded, sore, and frustrated, Flash was sure he was too slow to escape his coming doom. The barking sound rang out again, closer this time.

The blazing sphere rocketed right for his head. Instinctively, Flash shifted into speed mode and just ran flat out. A scarlet blur, he outpaced the projectile easily. Flash zoomed, putting serious distance between him and his hunters.

Until the pain gripped his muscles like a crushing fist and dropped him writhing into the dirt. The flaming shell exploded over his head. In the excitement he had forgotten his newfound curse, and it had nearly ripped him apart. With the still raw, hot agony throbbing through his system, Flash wasn't sure actually being shredded wouldn't be a relief.

The ape sentries thundered toward him, set on bagging their prey. Flash lay aching in the dirt, hidden by the weeds and brush around him, but only temporarily. Nearby, many small stones and rocks were scattered. Wrapping his red-gloved hands around a few of these, Flash became inspired. He couldn't use his speed to run, perhaps, but he could still access speed in other ways.

Flash crouched uncomfortably in the weeds, a good-sized pile of stones gathered within easy reach at his side. He whirled his arm in a superswift arc and fired a stone at the approaching gorillas.

As if released from a slingshot, the stone flew fast and hard to smash into the matted fur of one ape's blocky head. Startled, the ape stumbled and cried out in pain.

Before either gorilla could respond, a hail of rocks hurtled their way like bullets from an AK-47. The barrage of stones pummeled the apes mercilessly, driving them to their knees. They screamed in pain.

Flash rose, his sweeping arm still whisking stone after stone at his enemies. They might have been tough, but repeated shots to their craniums sent them quickly to a very painful dreamland. A scarlet-garbed David had easily taken out two hairy Goliaths armed only with stones and an unerring aim.

Flash left his fallen adversaries and headed for Gorilla City at a trot. He soon came to a clearing and saw something lying discarded in the weeds: Batman's Bat-binoculars, or whatever he called his viewing device. The Flash didn't want to think about what could have made Batman drop it, but holding the lenses up to his eyes, he quickly discovered that his questions about finding a way into the Gorilla's secret home had been answered.

Through the lenses, which were ultrasensitive to light wavelengths, Flash could see a glowing orange energy barrier. Not far away was a gap in the otherwise unbroken expanse.

"Thanks, Bats," Flash murmured. "I'll see to it you get these back, pal."

Flash entered Gorilla City cautiously. He anticipated conflict and had already devised several response options. He chuckled grimly to himself. He was finally thinking ahead and Green Lantern was nowhere around to be impressed. Flash hoped they'd both live long enough to celebrate this great leap in his personal development.

A long road paved with large octagonal slabs led from the gate into the city. No one was in sight, but Flash knew better than to assume he was alone. He moved stealthily from shadow to shadow, keeping close to the trees.

Several well-armed ape flunkies guarded the main building, but Flash could tell they weren't paying attention to the job. Bored, they grumbled and squabbled among themselves. All the same, Flash would have to go through them to gain entrance to the inner compound.

Not long ago he could have moved past them faster than any eye could follow. A breeze would have been the only evidence of his passage. But that time was past. Now, Flash reminded himself, he had to do this the hard—and human—way.

But he was not completely without speed. Flash stepped out onto the tiled walkway, calling to the gorilla warriors. Slowly, stupidly, they looked up, surprised at the appearance of an intruder. They practically fell over each other in the scramble to react.

From their vantage point, the ape guards saw only a tall, slim man in a red uniform and mask standing absolutely still. They could not see that his yellow-booted feet were moving at incredible, blurring speed.

Flash focused only on his task, ignoring the pain he could feel creeping into his leg muscles. He couldn't keep this up for long. Flash looked down to the walkway. The vibrations he was generating with his feet were beginning to transfer to the tiles. Flash shifted his position slightly and changed the focus of his constant vibration.

The tiles shook, then rattled, and finally began to jump. In a spreading wave of reaction, the vibrations rippled toward the startled guards, the large earthen slabs being swept along swiftly.

Suddenly, the apes fell back as the heavy tiles were blasted at them in a thundering tidal wave. Barraged by flying slabs, the gorillas were battered and soon flattened under the stream of pummeling paving.

Flash stopped in his tracks, his legs already throbbing painfully. He felt exhausted, but he couldn't rest yet. He had only begun his campaign against Gorilla Grodd's schemes.

Flash limped to the doors of the main pavilion, past the scattered forms of the unconscious guards. His body felt as though it were made of rigid, heavy concrete. *Focus past the pain,* he repeated over and over to himself. It almost worked.

At the massive doors, Flash listened for sounds of activity on the other side. He could hear only the distant drone of voices, nothing close by. He eased the door open and slipped inside silently. The speedster found himself in an open atrium, empty for the moment of any signs of life. Down a central concourse, he could still hear the droning voice.

"Grodd," Flash ground out.

In the vast council chamber Grodd busied himself by running his followers through pointless military exercises, lining them up first in one formation, then another. Grodd was bored, his troops were weary, and the spectators remained frozen in mental oppression.

The doors to the outer hall began to rumble and shake. Grodd and his guards looked up. What was this?

The wooden doors exploded inward in a pelting rain of splintering debris. Grodd's goons yelped in unified terror as their leader glared in disbelief at this bizarre intrusion.

"Who dares intrude?" Grodd bellowed.

"The guy who always mops the floor with your furry behind, Groddsie . . . me!" Flash said as he stepped fearlessly into the great hall. The speedster smiled his trademark impertinent smile.

Grodd stared in disbelief, rage bubbling in his eyes like boiling lava. Flash walked casually forward, looking around as if he hadn't a care in the world. His gaze fell on his trapped comrades, and while his heart sank in his chest at the sight, his light manner never flagged.

"Ah, collecting life-sized action figures, are you?" Flash smiled, gesturing toward the frozen Justice League.

"You *dare* face me alone—and *powerless,* you puny idiot?" Grodd sputtered.

"Ah, go eat a banana, monkey boy. Who says I'm powerless?"

Grodd glared, suddenly suspicious. Flash smiled derisively at the ape despot.

"The Weather Wizard shot you with the weapon I gave him. Your muscles are bound up in an unbreakable matrix of crushing energy!"

"That was *you,* eh?" Flash said. "Big surprise. Well, I ask you, if I were powerless could I do . . . *this*?"

Flash raised his arms and began to spin in place like a human top, going faster and faster, blurring into a spinning splash of scarlet. The whirling hero began to move into the room as Grodd ordered his guards to action.

"Stop him!" roared Grodd.

Flash's arms rotated like a propeller, punishing any ape who got too close. His whirling momentum scattered the gorillas like toys. Flash tore through the room like a human tornado. Grodd hopped and shook his huge fists, spitting in wild fury.

Flash felt the waves of pain pounding against his limbs. He was in trouble and knew it. He had to free his friends before his body seized up. His whirling form abruptly changed direction and headed for the imprisoned members of the Justice League. Grodd screamed orders to his battered forces.

In the end, none of apes laid a leathery finger on Flash. They didn't need to. In a sudden spasm of agony, Flash spun out of control. He skidded wildly across the floor to crash into the far wall, collapsing in a moaning heap, every fiber of his being ablaze with excruciating torment.

At Grodd's command, a squad of thugs fell on Flash's inert form and began to pound the fallen hero with abandon.

Flash was so far past caring or feeling that all of their punishing efforts were wasted. Grodd watched with grim satisfaction.

CHAPTER 9

Flash had no idea how long he had been unconscious. The pain that was his constant companion blurred his awareness considerably; he might have been out for a century . . . or a second.

In fact, it was the next morning when Flash opened his eyes and remembered his failure of the night before—his friends were still in Grodd's thrall. Flash winced in pain and shame. The ape maniac would get away with his mad scheme, and no one could stop him. Certainly, Flash had learned that *he* would not be the one to put Grodd down.

Flash looked around to find himself imprisoned within a glass cube. Outside, Grodd's loyalists milled around and looked at him with naked curiosity and overt contempt. A smile was too far beyond Flash's abilities, but he appreciated the irony all the same. He had been put in a zoo by gorillas.

Flash attempted to rise but could not. None of his muscles would respond; he was as helpless as an infant and about as powerful. Flash grimaced and closed his eyes; he had never known that he could hurt as much as he did right then. *Let them gawk,* Flash thought.

It had all depended on him. Flash chided himself for thinking he could take on any villain without his powers, let alone a monster like Grodd. It had been a nice idea that he might have had such a deep reserve of character and courage that he would save the day no matter what. That had been a naïve dream, and now he was wide awake.

Flash realized that it was all a joke. What he had inside was exactly nothing. Wonder Woman had gotten it wrong: he wasn't more than just his ability, he was far less. He had feared this awful truth all along but had tried to tough it out in hopes of saving his teammates. Now everything was worse, and he was a captive too.

If he'd been smart, Flash thought, he would have called in someone who could have actually helped.

Aquaman, perhaps, or one of the world's other heroes. Instead, he had tried to go it alone and blown it. If only Wonder Woman had been right . . .

The crowd of simian spectators outside his cell suddenly parted and moved away. Flash opened his eyes. Something big was coming. Or rather, he realized, some*one* big. Grodd.

Flash would not give the gorilla the satisfaction of seeing him flattened. With every ounce of will he could summon, Flash dragged himself to his feet, steadying himself against the dizzying pain and nausea that swept over him. He leaned as casually as he could against the translucent wall of his cage. He barely managed to look alive. His face was deathly pale, his expression was tight and drawn, and cold sweat ran down his back.

Flash and Grodd stared at each other. Flash stayed as steady as he could and did not blink. Grodd's face showed contempt and barely concealed amusement.

"It appears that you need someone to tell you when to lie down and stay dead, Flash," Grodd rumbled.

"And someone should tell *you* that you need the world's biggest breath mint," said Flash. "And that's *through* the glass!"

"Jeer on, buffoon. I know you are beaten . . . and *you* know it too."

Grodd gestured, and two of his apes stepped forward and swung open one end of the glass enclosure. Flash was too weak to do anything but watch. The two apes stepped in cautiously and took the hero by his arms. He did not resist.

"Take the fool outside. I have an entertainment tailored just for him."

"I've seen *Planet of the Apes*," Flash sneered. "Heck, I'm *living* it!"

"Shut up!" roared Grodd.

"Take your paws off me, you dang dirty apes!"

"We'll see how much you laugh, Flash," said Grodd, "as you watch your beloved Justice League being fed to the flames!"

Flash was dragged to a vast grassy plain beyond the buildings of Gorilla City. It looked like a field prepared for a tournament, and in a way it was. His captors tied Flash securely to a tree. From there, he could look out over the huge space. But why?

Already, a huge crowd of enthralled Gorilla City citizens was making its way out to watch whatever was

about to transpire. Another crowd of Grodd's followers was assembling as well.

Grodd himself strode as regally as his massive and
ungainly simian form could manage. Behind him a
large vehicle moved slowly. From Flash's limited
point of view, it looked something like a tank, with a
huge ray cannon situated atop the turret.

At the distant end of the flat grounds, Flash
could see a cluster of indistinct figures. He didn't
need to make them out clearly to know that it was
the Justice League. Flash began to see the developing
outlines of Grodd's vile intentions. It wasn't going to
be pretty.

Flash dropped his head, his pain so great that he
could barely focus on the moment. He was as helpless as a fly in a spider's web . . . but his teammates
were in even more trouble. They needed him, and
Flash wouldn't be able to raise even a feeble finger to
help. He grimaced. He was such a loser.

Grodd was suddenly standing at Flash's side,
gloating.

"I have to give you credit, speedster," Grodd said.
"You have come farther than I had anticipated
you would or could have. Your determination im-
presses me."

Flash tried to ignore the ape's sneering words, but they echoed in his ears.

"However, we both know that you're finished. The next time you use your speed, it will kill you—*if* you are even still capable of achieving any velocity at all."

Flash winced. The truth of his enemy's words burned in his heart.

"You have tried, but you have failed, Flash. Now, you will witness my utter—and ultimate—triumph over the Justice League!"

The huge tank thundered onto the plain, stopping to face the inert heroes, thousands of yards distant. The large chrome-and-glass barrel of the ray cannon swiveled to aim at the helpless targets. Already the ray device was humming as it built up its charge. A too-bright crimson glow emanated from the cannon's works. Flash stared at this sight with sick realization. Grodd smiled widely.

"That monstrous device is a laser cannon, Flash," said Grodd. "Its beam is as hot as the sun. It will easily reduce even Superman to ash."

"You don't have opposable thumbs, banana breath—there's no way you'll pull this off!" shouted Flash, but his taunts sounded hollow, even to his own ears.

"A laser beam moves at the speed of light, you know, Flash," said the villainous ape. "The only one fast enough to save them is *you*. But—oh!—your power will *kill* you if you try!"

Behind them, the cannon's hum built to a shrill whine as its power level intensified. In seconds, a beam of killing light would shoot out and destroy the Justice League. The Flash struggled weakly against his bonds.

"I love irony, don't you, Flash?" asked Grodd. "Only you could save them . . . if you were not forced to stand helplessly by while they are vaporized."

"Shut up!"

"I imagine that you must despise yourself for your weakness. After witnessing this horrific spectacle, you will no doubt long for your own demise."

Flash glared at Grodd. He said nothing.

"I will likely grant that desire, Flash, rest assured. But first you will watch your friends die."

Flash saw red; his breath came in short, ragged gasps, and his chest tightened painfully. He was every bit as helpless as Grodd said. There was nothing he could do to save them. The Justice Leaguers were going to die and he couldn't move to stop it. Again, he tugged fruitlessly on his stout bonds.

Grodd strode imperiously onto the field, his long arm raised.

"Prepare to fire on my signal," Grodd commanded.

"No! No!" Flash cried out. He surged pointlessly against the ropes.

The ray cannon was glowing with coruscating scarlet light. The barrel seemed almost molten with barely contained destructive fire. An earsplitting keening filled the air, and the whole tank shuddered with the buildup of power.

Grodd's arm dropped. The cannon fired. The intense ruby beam blasted forward at the speed of light.

Flash screamed. The beam blazed inexorably toward its target.

CHAPTER 10

The moment the laser was triggered, Flash's perspective shifted into super-fast awareness. What he saw was like a series of still images, one atop the other. The cannon glowed. A blazing beam inched forward. The beam stretched first several feet, then ten. Thanks to his speed, it would seem to take forever for the Leaguers to meet their inevitable doom.

Flash felt a strange vibration building within him. It was more powerful than anything he had ever experienced. He didn't know exactly what it was, but he loved the flood of power that surged through him as this vibration escalated.

He looked at Grodd, but the ape was as frozen as everything else. Only Flash seemed to be moving—and he *was* moving—to his own surprise. The exhilarating vibration had completely overtaken Flash's body. Pain seemed to melt away, as did the ropes that held him bound to the tree.

Flash felt himself float forward, feeling lighter and buoyed by the strange effervescent energy that erupted throughout his system.

The laser beam was like a still picture; now it had extended itself over about twenty yards. Flash flowed forward, swept along by this newfound swiftness.

There was a glitch in the smoothness of Flash's forward momentum as Grodd's speed-choking energy asserted itself. Distantly, the speedster was aware of pain, but it was as if that agony belonged to someone else. Flash blasted forward, still behind the laser beam but gaining quickly.

Flash's metabolism was rocked by wave after wave of crushing destructive energy, but it did not stop him. The pain hammered at the surging hero, like a gong timed to his racing heartbeat. The ravaging energy rent his nerves like ragged threads and smashed and shattered his molecules. The twisting, jagged power closed on his very being like a vise. Flash's atoms screamed in pain and violation. But still he raced on.

Racing ever faster, Flash moved beyond the pain,

slipping past and away from the deadly energy that was entwined in every aspect of his reality. As the speedster rushed onward, he could feel the crushing tightness loosening its grip. He was outracing Grodd's curse.

In awe, Flash looked down at himself as he zoomed; it was as if he could see through his own solid flesh. He watched the surging blue lightning ripping through his cells, but by now, he felt nothing. The rampant energy pulsed and writhed within him, but his own physicality was changing somehow. That energy was beginning to stream away in unfurling tatters.

He raced on effortlessly, the lancing beam still ahead. Flash felt lighter, almost immaterial. Everything he saw was haloed with brilliant, glittering scarlet light. Something was happening—it was if Flash was becoming pure speed. But what did that *mean*? And how was he doing it?

Flash seemed to be no more than red and gold smoke swept along by a super-swift wind. He blasted forward, drawing closer and closer to the beam.

Now Flash had lost all sense of his physical self. He felt more alive and powerful than ever before, but he still wondered if he was dying. Perhaps he had already died. Maybe he was a speeding ghost.

The crawling blue energy that bound his metabolism could not keep up; it was slipping harmlessly through the speedster's almost ethereal form. What little remained of it blew away in his wake like so much flashing blue exhaust. The energy had no more power over him; he was no longer the man who had been its unwilling host. He raced on and on, already as fast as light and accelerating even more.

Flash had transcended his body, leaving his corporeal form behind like a fading crimson memory. He had become an accelerating cloud of molecules, loosely bound by what little sense of self remained within.

Pain, fear, regret, and inadequacy were stripped away, replaced by an unstoppable strength of purpose. All that mattered was completing the mission at hand.

Save.

The.

Justice.

League.

The concept flashed word by word like neon within Flash's expanding awareness. He was an arrow, they were the target.

The laser beam was now only a dozen yards from

frying the trapped heroes, but Flash was only a few feet behind it. He surged forward, faster and faster. Flash could feel air rushing through his being as he raced on. His vision was transformed even further, every object starkly clear in its absolute stillness, but all was now surrounded by auras of vivid and shimmering red radiance. He no longer saw things in the normal three-dimensional reality; somehow, Flash could see what was ahead as if from multiple perspectives.

In what little self-awareness he had left, he idly wondered if he would ever be able to return to his physical humanity again. It would be worth it if he were to remain in this transformed reality forever. He had earlier exulted in the joy of his speed, but now he had become the speed. Now he felt the joy blazing through him like chain lightning.

As his ego vaporized in transit, he realized that none of those thoughts mattered. Flash didn't matter. Saving the Justice League was everything. Beyond completing that task, there was nothing else. Beyond that, the remaining piece of Flash's individual consciousness understood in a blaze of awareness, he would achieve completion. *But what did that mean?*

Ahead, the Leaguers stood frozen in the face of the oncoming beam of deadly scarlet heat. Flash was faster than the laser now—like a beam of light himself, Flash zoomed right at his friends. The six heroes stood, surrounded and contained within the coruscating scarlet light. They were not conscious, but on the level that Flash's power moved, there was some inexplicable communication. Flash was coming. His friends understood.

The energy that had been the Flash smashed into the frozen figures of his heroic teammates. His essence washed over them in exploding, crashing waves of pulsing, cascading power and light. The blazing speed-energy shattered the forces that held them bound; it revived and energized them, it pushed them to safety before they even knew what was happening. It whisked them away and out of sight. Then that fading scarlet radiance winked out completely. Only a shimmering residue in the air showed that anything had been there at all.

The sizzling laser beam hit the grass where the captive League had been only a millisecond before. The ground exploded in a ball of immense heat and fire, heaving and flashing immediately into ash and smoke. A deep, blackened trench and a deeper smoking crater were all that remained. Acrid haze filled the air.

From where Grodd stood, it appeared as though

his murderous plot had been wildly successful. He had vaporized the Justice League. He turned to gloat to his other captive—but Flash was gone. The ropes that had held him were tied exactly as they had been, but the super-fast hero had vanished. How . . . ?

"Where is the Flash?" bellowed the huge ape in rage.

"The Flash is gone," said the still dazed Wonder Woman. "He gave his life to save ours."

The Leaguers stood in the brush where the scarlet light wave had carried them. They were all still reeling from their ordeal and the realization of how they had been saved.

"I think you're right," said Superman gravely. "I have the vague impression that he became . . . pure light. At the last moment, he . . . he exploded into us and set us free."

"By the gods of Mars," said the Martian Manhunter. "I believe you are essentially correct—at least as far as we can grasp what has happened."

"Poor Flash," said Hawkgirl.

Green Lantern looked up and around, as if sensing some residual energy in the air like a static charge.

"No, don't feel sorry for him," said the Emerald Crusader. "The Flash did what he had to do. I'm sure he more than understood the risks."

"Yes, he was a hero," said the Amazon Princess. "This is what he was about."

"Whatever happened here, we shouldn't let his sacrifice be in vain," said Batman. "Grodd is still a major threat."

The sound of an ape's startled cry drew Grodd's attention back to the smoke-hazed field. Charging toward him were six colorful heroes, definitely alive, evidently well and frighteningly determined. Grodd could not understand how everything had gone so terribly wrong.

He had seen the accursed Justice League reduced to ashes. There was no way they could have escaped their fiery doom. Yet . . . here they came.

But how could this be? How could the unstoppable will of Grodd be so thoroughly routed?

There was only one possible answer, but it was even more impossible than the Justice League's survival.

"Flash!" snarled Grodd.

Though most of the gorillas were superintelligent, Grodd had very little trouble finding plenty of lesser apes willing to follow him without question. Granted, his psychic force suppressed their will, but Grodd also used his powers to reduce whatever personal intellect they possessed. They were stupid, perhaps, but loyal and incapable of ambition. When Grodd spoke, his troops acted.

There were roughly one hundred of these elite warriors. As Grodd watched the Justice League rushing to battle, his followers rallied immediately to his defense. His will was theirs; as quickly as the thought entered his powerful mind, it suffused theirs as well. The ape forces swept toward the heroes in a wall of massive, hairy muscularity to protect their beloved leader.

The Justice League was inundated with the swarming ape soldiers. Even Superman was driven back by the sheer force of numbers. None of the apes carried weapons—there were none immediately at hand; no one expected they would need weapons to watch the League's demise. This was sloppy, brutal, hand-to-hand combat.

At least a few of the Justice Leaguers were content to meet their foes in this earthy fashion.

Hawkgirl grabbed up a long, sturdy tree branch and used it as a club. Swinging it over her head like a fighting staff, she smashed one foe hard against his jaw, then reversed the staff into the gut of another. Two stunned apes fell away. Hawkgirl whirled her staff over her head like a propeller, clocking several other ape attackers.

Green Lantern used his ring to create a wedge-shaped plow blade. Pushing the massive construct forward like the prow of some great ship, the Emerald Crusader battered through a wall of simian resistance, lifting and tossing the stunned apes aside like discarded toys. Green Lantern focused his concentration and forced his huge blade to dig into the earth. He gashed a long, deep trench before them and proceeded to knock more attackers into the ragged tear.

Wonder Woman, a daughter of Amazon warriors, reveled in the combat. She cast her magical lasso, its loop expanding miraculously to encircle a group of eight charging apes. The glimmering golden rope cinched around the bulky, squirming creatures, constricting their ample stomachs. The apes fought this bondage for only a few seconds before being slammed hard into the ground, where they fell instantly into unconsciousness.

"Eight at once, nicely done," said Green Lantern. "A very efficient way to reduce the opposition's numbers."

Wonder Woman drove a fist into the face of a single gorilla assailant. She grunted with the effort, smiling just a bit. A loud, hollow *klonk* sounded at the impact.

"Thank you, but I'm not above the personal touch," said the Amazon.

Superman stood on a slight rise, amidst a grasping squad of gorilla soldiers. They punched and kicked and bit at him, but the invulnerable Man of Steel shook them off. He lifted an ape above his head with one hand even as he knocked two more aside with a sweep of his powerful, blue-clad arm. Laughing, the Metropolis Marvel tossed his raised foe across the field into another bunch of apes, and they went flying like bowling pins.

"Get the pointy-eared one," shouted an ape commander. "He is a mere human—he has no power!"

Batman only smiled at the idea of his helplessness.

Like a sower with seed, the Dark Knight tossed a handful of small silver spheres into the air in front of the charging pack of apes. Fascinated by the shining baubles, the gorillas stared upward at the spinning balls. That was their first mistake. The spheres suddenly exploded in blinding light with sharp, concussive reports. The apes grabbed at their stricken eyes and ears and stumbled, screaming in terror.

Four apes leapt at the jade giant, J'onn J'onzz, who stood calmly awaiting their attack. They fell upon him and began to pummel him with their huge fists. It took a moment for the apes to realize that their quarry was no longer beneath them. Worse still, all their powerful blows had landed only on each other. J'onn rose like smoke from the ground a foot away from his tangled antagonists. He had become immaterial and sunk away into the earth. He stared down on his teeming enemies with some pity. Using his telepathic abilities, the Manhunter beamed a thought bolt into their minds—knocking them out . . . from the inside.

The apes raged like huge angry children, reverting to their natural state: beating their chests, bellowing challenging hoots, roaring defiance. The heroes took every care to take the bestial attackers down as humanely as possible.

Grodd was no longer on the scene, having run away in panic moments before. As the six heroes finished off his guards, they found themselves facing an advancing wall of simian pawns. Grodd had mentally commanded his helpless captive apes to intercede and fight the heroes on his behalf. Leading the pack was Solovar, his vacant gaze lending the scene an eerie aspect.

The Justice League stopped as these apes surrounded them. They did not want to risk hurting these helpless puppets, but getting through them would prove difficult. Meanwhile, the heroes were sure, Grodd was planning to make everyone's life even more miserable.

In the council chamber serving as Grodd's throne room, the gorilla rebel charged toward his huge psychic generator. He needed to ramp up its output to increase his control. He might even be able to retake the minds of the accursed Justice League! Grodd cranked the controls on the device's face. The air crackled with wild power, and Grodd felt his mind open to this expanding mental field.

Soon, Grodd soothed himself, soon he would be back in control. Soon he would spread that control to all humanity. Then he would rule the world with physical and mental might.

But something was suddenly not right. The machine began to shake and bang. Its gleaming black surface crawled with antic bolts of yellow lightning energy. Grodd's fur rose stiffly in the charged air. His eyes were wide and white against his dark fur and darker expression.

The steel shell of the controlling engine ruptured and split with a loud, rending screech. It shook even more violently now; fire and foul smoke poured from its complaining works. Grodd staggered away, covering his head, as with a huge *WUMP* the amplifying engine exploded with incredible force and a pyrotechnic display of awesome scope.

Grodd picked himself up, shaken by the events and his loss of power. The wreckage of the machine burned brightly, still popping and hissing as it destroyed itself. The air buzzed with raw, loose energy.

Grodd jerked suddenly as some unseen force slammed him in the face. What was going on? A wind stirred inside the big room, Grodd's stiff fur ruffling in the inexplicable breeze.

Another blow from nowhere struck Grodd in his broad middle. He whuffed in pain.

"Who is it? What is going on?" screamed Grodd.

All at once, Grodd's bulk was peppered with countless painful punches—all from out of nowhere. The blows, like drops of water carving through granite over time, began to take their toll. Grodd bellowed with rage.

The huge gorilla fell clumsily backward. The blows continued to rain out of thin air to batter Grodd. He began to wonder if he was being haunted. Whatever his unseen attacker was, it did not seem to respond to his mental probes.

As he fell, Grodd felt himself being caught up and lifted as if by some incredibly strong wind. This wind swept Grodd across the room, only to stop abruptly.

Grodd shouted for his guards, but no one could hear him. Suddenly, while still suspended in midair, Grodd began to spin crazily, faster and faster. He whirled helplessly, his speed ever increasing. Grodd screamed.

Without warning, Grodd's trajectory changed yet again. This time, he went flying across the room to smash hard into his large thronelike chair. It splintered to fragments as the big ape cannonballed into it. Grodd crawled from the wreckage, his fur littered with wood shards and sawdust. His eyes were wild with fear and loathing.

An impossibly powerful punch landed on the ape's jaw, sending him spinning. Grodd sprawled in a heap. He raised his head, expecting more punishment—or a glimpse of his attacker. But Grodd was alone in this place. For the first time, the imperious gorilla genius was afraid for his life. Who had done this?

Another rush of wind swept around Grodd as he lay on the floor, huddling in fear and apprehension. He sneaked a glance upward and was staggered by what he beheld. His enemy revealed himself.

Flash stood over his fallen ape enemy, smiling. Grodd was beaten, his threat ended. With the machine wrecked, Solovar and the other gorillas would be free of Grodd's evil control. And Flash knew that his fellow Justice Leaguers were safe and alive.

Most interestingly, though, Flash had found himself returned to health after his earlier incredible transformation. He had no idea how any of it had happened; he only knew that he had awakened in the jungle, vaguely aware of what had transpired. A careful test revealed that the invasive energy that had held him in check was gone completely. He was free to run again.

Grodd stared in chagrin at the scarlet-suited hero above him. Once again the gorilla villain had fallen to the speedster's power.

Grodd groaned once and slid into unconsciousness. It was over; he had been beaten.

Flash smiled broadly as he speedily bound the hands and feet of the unconscious ape. It was good to be the big dog.

It was even better to be the *fast* one.

CHAPTER

12

In the end, Grodd's elaborately constructed schemes collapsed with surprising ease. Deprived of their leader—and his mental domination—the rebellious underling apes surrendered quickly. What remained of Grodd's mind control machinery was smashed. Life in Gorilla City was very quickly back to its serene norm.

The Justice League stayed on to help restore order and see to Grodd's incarceration. Solovar, ever the thoughtful and inspiring leader, expressed renewed hope that his recalcitrant constituent might someday be rehabilitated. But despite his optimism, Solovar understood that it would not be a swift process.

"Grodd's crimes were largely directed against us,"

Solovar said to the assembled Justice League. "With your permission, we'd like to see to his punishment ourselves."

Batman spoke for the League.

"Well, it seems evident that Gorilla City is uniquely qualified to handle such a rare and powerful prisoner. Unless Flash wants to press an assault case . . ."

"Yeah, I can see the big hairball in Central City lockup now, demanding his lawyer." Flash grimaced. "No offense, Solovar, but he's all yours."

In the passageway outside Solovar's office, the League members watched Grodd being taken to Gorilla City's containment center. The huge ape was strapped securely into a restraining steel frame, which was rolled along by two gorilla guards. A mind-damping helmet was fastened to the rebellious ape's head. The helmet did nothing to calm Grodd's seething fury, however.

"Blast you costumed fools, I will not forget this!" Grodd snarled.

"Actually, Grodd, you probably will. All part of the rehabilitation process . . . ," said Solovar, smiling mildly.

Flash strolled up to Grodd, grinning widely.

"Aww, I hope you don't forget *me*, Groddsie. I'm the fella who kicked your furry behind . . . again."

"You . . . you . . . I will kill you with my bare hands!" Grodd growled, staring at the speedster with a gaze that could cut diamonds.

Grodd put all of his focus into a mind blast aimed at the Flash, who merely smiled patiently. The helmet assured that Grodd's power was completely neutralized.

"No fun at all to have your style cramped, is it?" asked Flash. "That ugly hat has your brain completely on hold."

Grodd roared and ranted his frustration all the way to his cell. No one in Gorilla City paid the slightest bit of attention.

A short time later in a medical lab, Solovar supervised a crew of gorilla scientists in examining the Flash's metabolism. The speedster lay on a brightly lit table under a rolling scanning device. The ape physicians clucked and mumbled as they watched the numerous readouts and dials. The rest of the Justice League watched the watchers.

"What's the verdict, folks," Flash asked, "will I ever dance the Macarena again?"

Solovar and the scientists stared without comprehension. Green Lantern stepped forward with an expression of barely contained amusement.

"Ignore him, and be glad that humor doesn't always translate across cultural distance."

"But it would seem that Flash is showing every sign of improvement," said Superman with a smile.

"If you can call his jokes an improvement," Hawkgirl added.

Solovar nodded, looking pleased. He studied a scrolling data screen with satisfaction.

"The medical scans confirm our suppositions," Solovar said. "There is no trace whatsoever of Grodd's energy remaining in Flash's metabolism."

"What happened to it?" asked Wonder Woman.

"I can only guess," answered Solovar, "but I think he *outran* it rushing to your rescue earlier."

Flash stepped down from the examining table, curious and uncharacteristically serious for the moment.

"Yeah, about that . . . how did I do it? What happened to me out there?"

Solovar looked thoughtful as he considered the question. He really had no concrete answer for the Scarlet Speedster. What had happened should have been impossible. But the impossible was rather commonplace for the Justice League. Solovar spoke carefully, clearly still working out the answer for himself.

"I can only guess. Grodd managed to infiltrate your system with a disabling energy that, as you know, interfered with your ability to use your speed." Solovar paced the lab as he spoke. "I think the invasive power was keyed to the energy that grants you your speed in the first place—which your body generates in endless supply. In essence, the two energies acted like opposing magnetic charges. Where they conflicted, a storm of pain resulted."

Flash and his Justice League friends listened intently. Flash was embarrassed to realize how little he knew about his own power. It had been a gift, one he had accepted with gratitude, but the science of it was beyond him. Solovar continued.

"The body-mind interface in your use of superspeed is incredibly important, Flash. Your speed is your means, but it is your imagination and will that drives you."

"And occasionally," Flash added, "my appetite."

"Yes, that as well, I am sure," Solovar went on. "In any case, the strength of your will could not be constrained by the inhibiting energy, even if your speed was."

Flash looked at the faces of his friends as they listened to Solovar. He saw relief and fondness in their expressions. Flash smiled warmly; they liked him, they really liked him. To his credit, the speedster did not say this aloud. Maybe he was growing up.

"When your friends were in such dire need, your will overcame your body and pushed you to your utmost to save them. You went beyond even the agony of Grodd's imposed limitations." Solovar smiled at Flash.

"But what happened to me?" asked Flash, "It was as if I became a phantom. . . ."

Solovar shrugged his broad simian shoulders.

"Here we are even further from what science can adequately explain, I am afraid. In motion, your body is vibrating at an incredible rate. In many ways, I believe you are somewhat incorporeal whenever you speed."

Flash stared in confusion. This was news to him.

"Think about it," said Solovar. "An accelerating body will perforce encounter certain aerodynamic inevitabilities: wind resistance, momentum, drag . . . things you never encounter.

"In motion, your power allows you to move through space with no resistance at all. Momentum is never an issue; you can turn any corner, or stop literally on a dime."

Flash's expression showed the wonder of these possibilities. Solovar continued.

"You move as if within your own world, Flash— because you are not quite in this one when you speed. The faster you go, the more your vibrations take you out of sync with normal reality."

"So what keeps my molecules from just blowing away in the breeze?" asked Flash.

"Your speeding body is surrounded by a vibratory aura that maintains your physical integrity, it seems," said Solovar, "and this aura is subject to your will too."

"Pushed to the extreme, instinct took over and you vibrated so fast you shed Grodd's energy like water and saved us," the Martian Manhunter offered.

"Well, that's a theory, anyway," added Solovar. "In the end, you are the only real expert when it comes to your power."

"Great," said Green Lantern, "that means no one knows."

"It's simple," said Wonder Woman. "Everything you are comes from within you, Flash. From your heroic heart. Thanks to that, you are unstoppable."

"I hope that means you're warming up to the idea of a date, Princess," teased the Flash, "because, as you hear, I am definitely better than normal!"

"Perhaps, but apparently some things never change," said Wonder Woman. "Welcome back, friend."

The Justice Leaguers, with the exception of the perpetually taciturn Batman, laughed in relief and enjoyment. The Dark Knight had the last word.

"It's time we headed back. No doubt other menaces are already awaiting our attentions."

"Go in peace, friends," said Solovar. "Once again Gorilla City is in your debt."

"Good luck keeping Grodd on the leash," said Flash, "at least until you get him housebroken."

The Justice Leaguers said their good-byes and headed for home.

"Somebody do me the favor of piloting the *Javelin 7* back home, please," said Flash, "I'm traveling under my own power again!"

With that, Flash vanished in a blurring streak, leaving only a whipping breeze behind. The other heroes watched his departure with fondness.

"Our little speedster is all grown up," said Green Lantern with a smile.

"Well, almost," added Superman.

EPILOGUE

Flash zoomed across the ocean like a stone skipping across a pond. He moved so fast that the water's surface was as solid as concrete to him.

Once again, the Scarlet Speedster exulted in the use of his superspeed, perhaps even more so now that he had a better grasp of exactly what he could do with it.

The salt wind washed past him as he raced. Already the coast of the United States was visible on the distant horizon. The Flash leaned into his speed, increasing his velocity to an incredible degree. Now he was one with the rushing wind, moving faster and faster toward home.

As much as he was enjoying his exhilarating rush,

however, Flash found himself looking forward to relaxing with his feet up. He had earned a rest. The Flash smiled to himself; now that he was more mature, he was starting to think like an old man.

More than anything, though, he recognized another feeling driving him on now. A growing, rumbling emptiness was making itself loudly known within. This was something very familiar to Flash; it was obviously way past time for dinner. He poured on the speed and steered for land.

Soon, firm ground replaced salt water beneath Flash's feet. He zoomed up a highway, past cars that seemed to be standing still. Night was coming on, and the lights glittered in beautiful, streaming streaks as they came to life. The Flash looked down at himself in curiosity, seeking any sign of change. He seemed, to his own perception, to be perfectly normal and quite solidly real. Maybe Solovar had been wrong.

The Flash considered all the amazing things he had heard and weighed them in his mind. He was no scientist, but he did have an innate sense of what he could and could not do. As bizarre and extreme as

Solovar's theories seemed, Flash had to admit that everything the ape had said sounded right. It felt right as well. The Flash was master of his super-speed and his metabolism. Who knew what more he could learn to do?

All he knew for certain at that moment was that he couldn't think too hard on an empty stomach. The Flash veered across the busy highway and exited, following signs for restaurants ahead.

Soon Flash found himself speaking loudly into a big plastic bear's smiling mouth.

". . . three double cheese and bacon burgers and a colossal fries," said Flash. "And two chocolate shakes, please."

The bored teenager at the pickup window was startled to see that his customer was not in a car. It took a full ten seconds before it dawned on the kid that the customer was wearing a bodysuit in bright scarlet and gold.

"Welcome to Benny's. . . . Flash, what are you doing *here*?"

"To the victor go the spoils, pal . . . ," said Flash, hefting the waiting sack of steaming food, "and believe me, I've earned this!"

The dumbfounded clerk could only stare at the

ten-dollar bill that drifted on the sudden breeze into his open palm. The Scarlet Speedster was already long gone.

"Whoa, how about that, the Flash likes *fast* food!"

Flash laughed as he ran. Absolute joy poured over him like a deliciously warm shower. He knew he was more than his speed. He understood that he could survive without his power; maybe he would even continue to keep fighting the bad guys.

But he knew one thing for sure. The Flash enjoyed his speed more than he could ever explain. And he was ecstatic that he had reclaimed it and defeated Grodd. He smiled widely. He loved life in the fast lane.

The Flash zoomed toward home, spurred on by the seductive scent of cheeseburgers and french fries.

ABOUT THE AUTHOR

BRIAN AUGUSTYN was born and raised in Chicago, where he first discovered a love for comic books that continues to this day. After realizing that the odds against his personally developing superpowers were long, Brian turned his mind to envisioning the adventures of his favorite characters instead. He's been an editor and writer for many comics over the last eighteen years, having the great pleasure of steering the lives of many comics favorites, including the Flash. Brian lives with his ever-patient wife, Nadine, and two wonderful daughters, Caroline and Allison, in Connecticut.

frozen buildings.
chemical spills.
robot umbrellas.

just another night in gotham city...

Join Batman For Two <u>NEW</u> CD-ROM Action Mysteries.

COMING IN SEPTEMBER 2003!

Uncover the clues. Crack the case. Foil the fiends.

Available wherever computer games are sold, at www.learningco.com, or by calling 1-800-822-0312

The Learning Company®